Twelve Kinds of Ice

TWELVE KINDS

by Ellen Bryan Obed

OF ICE

Illustrated by Barbara McClintock

HOUGHTON MIFFLIN BOOKS FOR CHILDREN

HOUGHTON MIFFLIN HARCOURT

BOSTON NEW YORK 2012

Houghton Mifflin Books for Children is an imprint of

Houghton Mifflin Harcourt Publishing Company.

www.hmhbooks.com

The text of this book is set in Garamond BE.

The illustrations were created with pen and ink

on Arches cold press watercolor paper.

Library of Congress Cataloging-in-Publication Data is on file.

ISBN 978-0-618-89129-0

Manufactured in Singapore

TWP 10 9 8 7 6 5 4 3 2 1

4500371107

THE FIRST ICE

The first ice came on the sheep pails in the barn—a skim of ice so thin that it broke when we touched it.

The Second Ice

The second ice was thicker. We would pick it out of the pails like panes of glass. We would hold it up in our mittened hands and look through it. Then we would drop it on the hard ground to watch it splinter into a hundred pieces.

The Third Ice

The third ice was the ice that would not break. We hit it with the heels of our boots. We tapped it with the handle of an old rake. But the ice stayed firm.

My sister and I had heard it coming the night before. We lay in our beds, listening to the cold cracking the maple limbs in the yard. We had seen it coming in the close, round moon. We felt it coming through the windows onto our quilts. We had gone to sleep talking about the ice that would not break, because it was this ice that would bring us what we were waiting for . . .

$\mathcal{F}$IELD $\mathcal{I}$CE

The morning field ice came was like no other. Ice froze upon our day, and at school we could not think clearly—math and geography and reading were frozen solid. All day long we talked about our first skate, and on the way home from school we pressed our faces against the windows on the bus to look at the field ice. The one who saw it first was making the most important announcement of the year.

When the bus stopped in front of our house, we raced up the driveway and inside for our skates. We ran down to the neighbor's field, where a narrow strip of ice was waiting for us. Never mind the hay stubble sticking up everywhere. Never mind the small space. Never mind the first arguments between hockey sticks and figure skates. Never mind. Field ice was short-lived but glorious. It also spoke of . . .

Stream Ice

If the nights continued cold, stream ice came quickly after field ice. Dad took us in the car up the road to the stream where we had fished for trout in the spring. We sat down on its hard brown bank to tie up our skates. Then we followed Dad as he followed the stream. Sometimes we'd stop and lie down on our stomachs. We'd put our eyes close to the ice to watch the little fish and slender reeds moving in the cold current of the streambed. Then we'd follow Dad again until the stream smalled to a brook of bent alders. We followed him into the frozen thicket. We tried to see how far we could skate between branches, over stones, and around old logs. All afternoon the stream was ours until it was time to take off our skates and walk back to the car. All the way home we talked about . . .

Black Ice

Black ice is water shocked still by the cold before the snow. For black ice, Dad took us in the car a half-hour's ride to Great Pond, where on our summer dock we tied up our winter skates. We could see the clouds, the blue sky, the tree-edged shoreline, in the mirror of black ice beneath us. We could see ourselves in the glass, our long-winged spirals, our flashing blades, our new mittens. We skated around islands and in and out of coves. We looked beneath the ice and saw what we could not see in summer—boulders and cracks between boulders, black shadows and sunken tree branches. And we saw what was not there—the sullen backs and open jaws of hibernating monsters rising up from the lake bottom.

We made huge backwards circles and listened to the sharp cuts of our blades. We skated out to the middle of the lake—the forbidden place of frothing whitecaps in the summer. We could hear the ice cracking and groaning as it stretched itself in the cold.

We sped to silver speeds at which lungs and legs, clouds and sun, wind and cold, raced together. Our blades spit out silver. Our lungs breathed out silver. Our minds burst with silver while the winter sun danced silver down our bending backs.

We sped one mile, two miles, four miles, down the lake on a day of black ice and silver. Black ice, black shadows, black shores, black islands.

Silver blades, silver speeds, silver sun.

But black ice did not stay. As suddenly as it had come, it disappeared under the cover of the first snow. With the first snow came the time for . . .

Garden Ice

What was our vegetable garden in summer became our skating rink in winter. We made it with boards and snow, a garden hose, and hours of work.

In October, after the frost had killed the last of the plants, we cleared the garden of rock and root and withered stalk. We raked the surface until it was level. Dad would lie down on the ground to check for holes and little hills. Then we would rake some more. We put stakes at the four corners of the garden and connected them with a string. We carried the long rink boards that lay piled beside the barn to the edges of the garden. We nailed them to stakes hammered into the ground along the string. Then we waited for the cold to freeze the ground, and we waited for snow.

When the snow came, we began making garden ice. The first step was snow packing. Everyone worked on this—Dad and Mom, my brothers, my sister, and I. We stamped and packed the snow hard with our boots and shovels. We packed it with our skis. We packed it with the toboggan, on which one or two of us sat to be pulled back and forth across the hardening surface.

Suddenly, Dad would say, "Time to get the hose!"

When it was my turn, I'd run inside the house to the cellar stairs, turn on the light, and descend into the dark-shadowed cellar. The garden hose was curled up by the water tank, a long black snake with its nozzle mouth. Dad was waiting by a small hole cut beside the sealed cellar window. I passed the snake's nozzle mouth into Dad's gloved hands. As Dad pulled, I uncurled the black rubber snake, making it easy for it to slide up and out through the hole. When the hose was completely outside, I'd hear the muffled call, "Ready!" This was my signal to turn on the faucet.

Dad sprayed water lightly on the snow while we continued to stamp and pack. Soon ice patches began to form. We worked until we had to give the surface time to freeze solid. One of us would go inside to turn off the hose and pull it back into its nesting coil beside the water tank.

We continued these ice-making sessions after supper, just before bed, and early in the morning for several days until there it was—garden ice. But

by then, we didn't call it garden ice. We called it . . .

Bryan Gardens

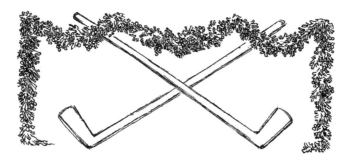

It was our Boston Garden, our Maple Leaf Gardens, our Montreal Forum. Bryan Gardens had lights and music; it had stands; it had schedules; it had hockey games and an ice show. It had rink managers; it had a locker room; it had fans. It had just about everything that the great arenas had except a roof. But Bryan Gardens had the sky, and to us, that was the best roof of all.

When Bryan Gardens was ready, it was one hundred by fifty feet of beautiful ice. And when Bryan Gardens was ready, the whole neighborhood knew. The school bus passed our place going up the hill so everyone could see the ice's glassy surface shining in the sun.

"The rink is ready!" spread from house to house up and down the road. *Everyone* was planning to skate—boys with old hockey sticks and new skates, girls with freshly sharpened figure skates, little brothers and sisters with their first skates. *Everyone* was planning their hours on the ice. But when Bryan Gardens was ready, so were the . . .

RULES OF THE RINK

Bryan Gardens
~ Rules of the Rink ~

1. Figure Skating: 3:30 - 4:30
2. Hockey: 4:30 - 5:30

3. No pucks on rink during figure skating.

4. Sweep the ice after skating (Boys and girls take turns.)

5. No skates in Kitchen without skate guards.

These rules were easy to keep at the beginning of
the season because everyone was excited to be on
the rink again. But it wasn't long before the boys
would get impatient waiting for their hockey hour
to come. They would put on their skates early and
sit on the snowbanks beside the rink. They would
watch the girls skate and occasionally toss a puck

onto the ice. One of the boys would retrieve the puck with long, winding glides around the figure skaters. It was time to knock on the window for the rink manager.

Mom would come to the door of the shed and announce, "An extra five minutes for figure skating!" When the figure skating hour was over, the boys leapt onto the ice like steers out of pens at a rodeo. They made sudden stops and starts; they smacked pucks against the boards; they circled forward and backwards. Soon they were lost in a tangle of sticks and arms and legs and voices.

Meanwhile, the girls were in the shed, taking off their skates. The shed was attached to the house.

We could open the kitchen door and be in . . .

The Locker Room

Large elm stumps were scattered about for seats. Skate guards, hockey tape, scraps of rag for wiping blades, an odd mitten, a stray sock, lay about the floor. Old skates and extra laces hung from the beams. Battered hockey sticks stood in racks along the sides of the room. Brooms and scrapers stood in one corner while huge shovels called "scoops" stood in another. Photos of our skating idols were taped to the walls.

The locker room was where we put on our skates and took them off again. It was where we talked about our jumps and spins and figure eights. It was where we planned our ice show and dreamt of being in the Olympics someday. It was also where we argued about whose turn it was to sweep the ice so that it could be ready for . . .

FLOODING

After supper when we were doing our homework
and Mom was putting our youngest brother to bed,
Dad would go out to flood the rink. He would
spray water over the marks and ruts and holes that
had appeared from a day of skating on Bryan Gardens. But first he would have a short skate of his
own. He would do tricks for our little brother, who
was watching with Mom at the upstairs window. We
could hear them laughing harder and harder until
we would leave our homework to join them at the
window. We crowded close together to watch Dad,
and when he was done, we knocked on the window
for more.

These were some of Dad's tricks:

Waltzing around the ice with a broom, pretending
it was his skating partner.

Accidentally tripping near the edge of the rink and falling headfirst into a snowbank, then waggling his feet up in the air and emerging with his head covered with snow.

Running or walking on his skates right off the rink as if nothing were wrong.

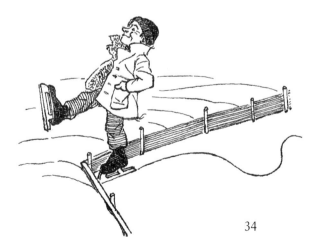

Spraying water from the hose up into the air, taking off his cap and holding it under the spray, and pretending to drink the water from his cap.

Dad loved flooding the rink. He loved the quiet night, the friendly stars, the clear cold. He wore huge, heavy gloves and a tired, tattered coat with a fur-lined collar pulled up to his hat. When Dad flooded, he grasped the hose as an artist does his brush. He sprayed water over the rink as an artist applies paint to his canvas. He worked for a masterpiece of ice, until one night, there it was . . .

Perfect Ice

Dad had worked hard and it was done—a one-hundred-by-fifty-foot surface of perfect ice.

No holes, no bumps, no ruts, no scratches.

And when Dad had his masterpiece of perfect ice, we knew it was time for . . .

A Skating Party

We had many skating parties at Bryan Gardens, but the best one was when Dad would invite students from the nearby college where he worked. He would make a small bonfire near the rink for roasting marshmallows and warming cold hands. Mom would make a huge pot of cocoa and bowls of popcorn for everyone when they came in from skating. But what we liked best about these parties was that we could skate better than most of our guests. We loved to dodge in and out as some of the college students staggered on skates for the first time or limped along on borrowed skates. When there was a little space between skaters, my sister and I would do a spin to show off. We liked the flirting games of tag and the scary momentum of crack-the-whip.

Music was piped out through a loudspeaker from an old record player in the shed—John Philip Sousa marches, Strauss waltzes, Rodgers and Hammerstein musicals.

We loved skating parties, but there was something we loved even more. It was a . . .

Late-Night Skate

After homework was done, after Dad had flooded, after lights were out in neighbors' houses, my sister and I would sometimes go out for a skate. Late-night skates were more exciting than daytime skates. We were alone with our dreams. We would work on our figure eights. We would work on our jumps and spins. We would put on music and pretend we were skating before crowds in a great stadium. We would try out moves that we'd seen figure skaters doing on television or in a picture in the newspaper. We were planning and practicing for some distant Olympics. We also were planning and practicing for . . .

Whoops!

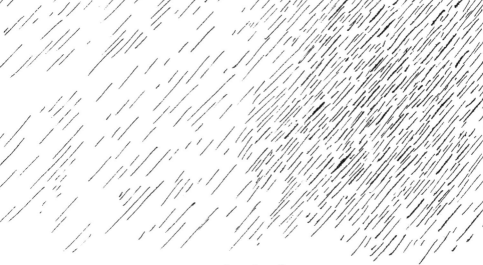

We were not planning for . . .

A Thaw

Right in the middle of a stretch of perfect ice, we would often have a thaw. The rain and warm temperatures lasted three or four days. Then it would turn cold again.

Once every few years we had a thaw that turned so quickly cold again that a heavy crust of ice formed on top of the snow. When this happened, we would beg to stay home from school to skate on . . .

Pasture Ice

With pasture ice our world became a skating rink. We skated out the door and across the front lawn. We zigzagged through the orchard around the sleeping apple trees. We climbed the fence and made wide circles in the sheep pasture before gliding down the hill in our neighbor's field.

Once, my sister's skate blade caught in a weak spot—she fell, knocked her wind out, and couldn't get up for several minutes. But this didn't stop us. We sailed over pasture ice all morning until the shiny crust weakened. We went back to the rink then, and to our plans and practices for . . .

THE ICE SHOW

The Bryan Gardens ice show was the event of the year. We planned it for school vacation, the third week of February. We called it "Icicles" (spelled differently each year according to who wrote up the program). "Icicles" had figure-skating acts, clown acts, and a grand finale called "Shower of Stars." We made costumes. We had programs and charged admission. We even sold refreshments.

Mothers and little brothers and sisters came. Fathers took time off from work, and our grandparents even drove all the way from New York to see the ice show. They sat on elm stumps by the side of the rink or on boards from old college bleachers that we placed on top of the snowbanks.

My sister and I were the directors of the ice show, and we planned a part for everyone. There were pair skating acts and solos. There were clown acts. Those who did not want to skate could choose to do something else—handle the record player and the music, sell refreshments, take admission, give out programs, or be the announcer.

One of the highlights of the show was Dad's clown act. Every year he had some of the same old tricks, but every year he had a new one, something better and more ingenious than the year before. One year it was the pail trick. He had two pails on the ice, one with water, one without. He'd skate by the crowd, showing them the pail with water in it. He'd go back to the empty pail. He'd pretend that it, too, was heavy and full of water. Then he'd motion toward the audience as if throwing water. Of course, it was empty, but the crowd would duck and shriek.

One year Dad skated around the ice with a lemon pie in his hand that Mom had made for the pie trick. He gestured to the crowd, asking if anyone would like a taste. Our grandfather from New York came close to have a better look. When he did, Dad put the pie right in his face.

When the ice show was over, we knew that the Bryan Gardens skating season was almost over, too. The late-February sun was warming the soil under the ice. Oozing yellow sun spots were beginning to form. Every day we skated on a smaller rink. Soon dirt patches appeared. And Dad would be carefully . . .

Counting Ice

Dad had a rink calendar on which he marked an *x* for each day of skating on Bryan Gardens. Late in the season when the rink was melting, he would have to decide whether the day could be counted as a skating day. We would have family discussions at the supper table. Could Dad mark an *x* on the calendar today? Had there been enough ice to skate? What about just enough ice for a spin? What about a day when we could skate for only an hour after the sun came up before the ice was covered with puddles?

We all had our say, but Dad made the final decision. The hardest counting decision Dad ever had to make was the year that Bryan Gardens had

ninety-nine days of skating. We worked very hard for the hundredth day, but the sun had won. After that winter, everyone who knew about Bryan Gardens knew about the year of ninety-nine days of skating. The very end of the season was called the time of . . .

THE LAST ICE

The last ice had grainy places that were like coarse sugar. Dad called this "punk ice." It also had hollow spots where our skates would break through. We had to skate carefully; the ice was almost gone.

Then, suddenly, it *was* gone. Lost mittens and stray pucks emerged from sunken snowbanks. A broken hockey stick appeared. A lost skate guard. And mud. Whenever we looked out the kitchen window or went by on the school bus, we would say, "The rink looks sad." Except for the rink boards, Bryan Gardens had completely disappeared.

Yet there was one more ice . . .

DREAM ICE

This ice came in our sleep. We never knew when it would come, but when it did, we could skate anywhere we wanted—down roads, in and out of yards, and over the tops of trees. We could do any jump we pleased without practicing. Double axels over houses and splits over telephone wires. We did spins on chimney tops and spirals down slanting roofs. We lifted off our skates into the sky to land on the back edges of clouds.

We never fell. We never got dizzy. We never got tired.

Dream ice never melted. We could skate on it in the springtime when we were planting the first rows of peas in the garden. We could skate on dream ice on hot summer evenings when we were watering the carrots and picking the beans. We could skate on it through the autumn, when we were pulling up tangled pumpkin vines and tough cornstalks.

We could skate on it until the first ice came again—a skim on the sheep pails—a skim so thin, it broke when we touched it.